THUD & BLUNDER

Raintree is an imprint of Capstone Global Library Limited, a company incorporated in England and Wales having its registered office at 264 Banbury Road, Oxford, OX2 7DY – Registered company number: 6695582

www.raintree.co.uk
myorders@raintree.co.uk

Edited by Julie Gassman
Designed by Steve Mead
Original illustrations © Capstone Global Library Limited 2017
Illustrated by Pol Cunyat
Production by Steve Walker
Originated by Capstone Global Library Limited
Printed and bound in China

ISBN 978 1 4747 2459 3
20 19 18 17 16
10 9 8 7 6 5 4 3 2 1

British Library Cataloguing in Publication Data
A full catalogue record for this book is available from the British Library.

THUD & BLUNDER
THE NOT-SO-EVIL WIZARD

Written by
SEAN TULIEN

Illustrated by
POL CUNYAT

raintree

a Capstone company — publishers for children

Thud is the daughter of the town's blacksmith. She's skilled with a hammer, whether she's pounding out dings in Blunder's armour or thumping a monster. Thud is equal parts brains and brawn!

THE TOWER & FOREST

What **Blunder** lacks in size and smarts, he makes up for in foolishness. He fearlessly charges into danger, whether it's real or not. He wields his mighty broad sword and never backs down from a monster.

MAP OF THE WORLD

MOUNT MOUNTAIN

NOT-SO-DARK
DUNGEON

VILLAGE
TOWN

OPEN
FIELD

CASTLE
KIDNAPT

CHAPTER 1

OINK! BAH! MOO-LA-LA!

It's the year Twelvity-Five A.D., in the town of Village Town. Thud and Blunder, two nine-year-old knights, have always searched far and wide for adventure.

But on this particular day, adventure finds them . . .

CLANG!

    CLANG!

        CLANG!

Thud hammered a red-hot slab of metal against an anvil. Slowly but surely, it began to take the shape of a sword.

Blunder sat nearby, watching Thud work the metal. "You should add spikes to it," he suggested.

Thud smirked. "You want to add spikes to everything," she said.

Blunder frowned. "Don't you?" he asked.

A strange sound interrupted Thud's work. She set down her hammer and glanced toward the town square.

The entire town square was filled with flying pigs, singing cows, and villagers who'd been turned into sheep!

"MOO-LA-LA!" the cows sang.

"OINK! OINK! OINK!" the flying pigs squealed.

7

"BAH! BAH! BAH!" the clothed sheep cried.

And in the middle of it all, running in circles and sending feathers flying every which way, was a talking rooster. "Oh, me! Oh, my!" he cried. "Please help me!"

Thud frowned. "That rooster has teeth," she said.

Blunder scratched his head. "Weird."

Thud and Blunder's eyes met. "Are you thinking what I'm thinking?" Thud asked.

Blunder smiled. "Seem like an adventure awaits!" he said.

They hurried to the back corner of the shop. Thud removed three loose planks from the floor to reveal two sets of armour below. A large sword lay atop the suits. A shield and a heavy hammer lay to the side.

In moments, the two nine-year-old adventurers were armoured up and wielding mighty weapons!

Thud emerged from the shop, hefting her hammer in one hand. She held her shield with the other.

Blunder brought up the rear, dragging his not-at-all-too-big sword behind him.

"You there!" Blunder said to the rooster. His voice was twice as big as his sword. "What is going on here?"

The rooster froze. His tiny eyes bulged. "Are the two of you . . . adventurers?"

"My name is Blunder," Blunder said. "And this is my sidekick, Thud."

Thud rolled her eyes. "I'm not his sidekick," she said. "But yes, we are adventurers."

The rooster held his wings together as if thanking the heavens above. "Oh, thank the heavens above!" he said.

He lowered his rooster head, wattle and all, and slumped his feathered shoulders. "My name is Bard, and I was once an adventurer like you – until an Evil Wizard changed everything . . ."

Thud leaned on her hammer. "How did you know he was evil?" she asked.

Bard tilted his head. "Duh," he said. "The word **Evil** is in his very name!"

Blunder nodded. "Good point."

Thud rolled her eyes.

Bard flapped his wings. His tiny eyes burned into Blunder's, telling a silent tale of bitter rage and woe.

"Please make the Evil Wizard turn me back to a human," Bard begged.

Bard quickly held out his wings, gesturing to all the animals (and villagers) around him. "Only you two adventurers can save us all!"

Blunder blushed. He thrust his sword into the air. "I, Blunder, vow to smite this Evil Wizard of Evil in the name of adventure!"

"I am so relieved!" Bard said with a sigh of relief. "The worrying was eating me alive."

Blunder chuckled. "That reminds me," he said. "It's lunchtime. How about chicken salad sandwiches?"

"How dare you!" the rooster squawked. He glared at Blunder.

"Leave him be," Thud said. "He's suffered enough." Thud turned to face the tiny rooster. "Sir, we would never eat you – no matter how long our journey is."

Bard took a step back. His beady eyes looked left and right. "Thanks . . . I think," he said.

Then, with surprising speed, Bard darted off to the west. "Follow me!" he called. "Adventure is this way!"

Thud and Blunder eagerly ran after the toothy rooster.

CHAPTER 2

OFF TO BEAT THE WIZARD

The three adventurers stood at the edge of a deep, dark forest.

"It looks deep," Blunder said.

"And dark," Thud added.

"And deadly!" Bard said. "But it's the only way to reach the Evil Wizard's Tower of Evil. So follow me . . . and keep your eyes open!"

The two nine-year-old knights followed the rooster into the forest.

Eerie sounds tickled their ears as they passed through the shadows. Strange shapes shifted just out of sight.

Suddenly, three Evil Monsters appeared!

"Gobble-gobble-gobble!" came their battle cry.

Blunder screamed and drew his sword. "Kill them before they eat us!"

Thud held Blunder back. "Not so fast," she said.

Bard giggled. "They're just Wild Turkeys, Blunder."

Blunder lowered his sword. "I knew that."

The brave adventurers followed Bard further into the forest.

As they walked, eerie sounds whispered into their ears. Unsettling shapes danced in the corners of their vision. Suddenly, three more Evil Monsters appeared!

"GOBBLE-GOBBLE-GOBBLE!"
came their battle cry.

Blunder raised his sword and charged.
"DIE, EVIL MONSTERS!" he cried.

Thud held Blunder back. "Not so fast," she said.

Bard explained. "These Wilder Turkeys are also harmless, Blunder," he said.

Blunder lowered his sword. "I knew that," he lied.

Blunder followed Bard and Thud even further into the forest.

The eerie sounds soon stopped. The shadows were still.

Blunder shivered. "I liked it better when it was noisy," he said bravely.

"Me too," Thud said. "Bard, would you sing us a tale of adventure?"

No answer came. Thud and Blunder looked left and right, up and down.

"B-bard?" Blunder said, trembling with bravery. "Where are you?"

Suddenly, an Evil Monster appeared! The beast wore armour, and it carried a club covered in spikes.

"I'LL **GOBBLE-GOBBLE-GOBBLE** YOU UP!" came its battle cry.

Blunder grunted. "Ha. Just another harmless turkey," he said. He walked right past it.

"GOBBLE?!" the armoured and club-carrying turkey said. It swung its weapon at Blunder's back!

Thud sprinted at Blunder and pushed him out of the way just as the club's spikes whistled past them. **WHUMP!**

The weapon smashed into the earth mere inches away from where they lay.

The two friends stared at the huge crater left by the weapon's impact.

"That's an Evil Monster, isn't it?" Blunder said flatly.

"Yes," Thud said more flatly.

"It's the Wildest Turkey!" Bard shouted from behind Thud and Blunder.

Thud and Blunder looked up at the not-so-harmless Wildest Turkey. Its coxcomb mohawk trembled with turkey rage.

Then it raised its weapon and let out
a **GOBBLE-GROWL!**

Thud looked at Blunder. Blunder
looked at Thud.

"Run!" Thud shouted.

Blunder grabbed Bard by the legs,
and he and Thud bravely ran away.

CHAPTER 3

THE EVIL TOWER OF EVIL

After several minutes of heroic fleeing, the adventurers reached the far side of the Wild Forest.

Bard smoothed his feathers. "That was a close call."

Blunder looked over his new bruises. "I hate running away," he grumbled.

"Me too," Thud said. "But we live to adventure another day."

"The adventure has yet to begin," Bard said. He gestured grandly with one of his wings. "Behold . . . the Evil Tower of Evil!"

Thud smirked. "Is it Evil?" she asked.

Bard nodded gravely. "With a capital **F**," he said gravely.

Bard scurried toward the tower. "Follow me!" he said.

Thud made a face. **"F?"** she said to Blunder. "There's no **F** in **Evil**."

Blunder shrugged. "Adventure is not a spelling contest, Thud," he said.

Thud chuckled. "I guess not," she said.

Upon entering the tower, Thud and Blunder gazed upwards. An endless spiral of stairs loomed above them.

"I am *not* climbing those," Thud said.

"Me neither," Blunder said.

"Fear not!" Bard said. "I know a magical shortcut."

TAP! Bard tapped his beak on a dirty spot on the wall.

WOOSH! The wall slid away to reveal a secret room.

Blunder walked inside the shiny metal room. "Ooh!" he cooed. "What is this thing?"

"It's called a Magical Transportation Device," Bard said. "It will take us all the way to the top of the tower!"

"Ooh," Blunder cooed.

"How does it work?" Thud asked, stepping inside.

"It uses magic to transport people and things," Bard said. He waddled over to a panel on the wall.

PLOK! Bard poked his beak into a button with a sideways **8** on it. The doors magically closed.

"Wait," Thud said. "How did you know about this thing?"

BING! The Magical Transportation Device began to move.

"Going up!" Bard said, ignoring Thud's question.

The three adventurers went up and up and up. Bard worked hard to not make eye contact with the two young knights.

Eventually, the Magical Transportation Device's door slid open with a **BING!**

They entered a circular room filled with bookshelves.

An old man sat at a desk in the rear of the room. He was hunched over a very big, very old book.

A silly, floppy hat covered his messy white hair. A less silly and less floppy robe covered him from neck to toes. A scraggly, and not silly or floppy, white beard hung from his chin.

"Um, hello?" Thud said.

The Evil Wizard looked up from his work. Upon seeing the intruders, his eyes began to crackle with magical energy. "Leef now!" he said.

Blunder raised his hand. "What?" he asked.

The Evil Wizard's long beard trembled with magical might. **"LEEF!"** he repeated.

Thud frowned. "What?" she asked.

Bard ducked behind Blunder's legs.
"Don't let him speak! He'll cast an **EVIL**
spell on you."

Blunder raised his pointy sword at the
Evil Wizard. "Prepare for pointy justice!"
he cried.

FOOSH! The Evil Wizard began to
float! "I wahnd you . . ." he said.

Thud and Blunder took a few steps back as the hovering Evil Wizard hovered. He held his hands in the air and wiggled his fingers. His eyes swirled with darkness. The very air around him seemed to shimmer with fear.

VOOM! A rip in space, time, or space-time (or something) appeared in front of the young knights!

Eerie cries echoed out from the strange hole.

Thud and Blunder raised their weapons. They braced themselves for the arrival of what would surely be an Evil Monster of nightmarish Evil.

In a booming voice, the Wizard chanted, "I catht a thpell for . . . EVIL MONTHTERTH!"

The portal shivcred and shimmered. And then . . .

MEW! MEW! MEW! Furry little animals flew forth from the portal!

Blunder was covered with kittens. They clung to his armour, purring and mewling.

"Kitties!" Thud cried. She dropped her hammer and scooped one up.

The kittens licked Blunder's face and crawled all over him. "Thud . . . are kittens evil?" he asked.

BOOP! Thud gently tapped a kitty on the nose. "Definitely not," she said.

While Thud and Blunder pet the kittens' soft fur and listened to them purr, the magical energy faded and the portal closed.

With a sigh, the Wizard sank back to the floor. "Anothuh mithpell," he said.

Thud set the kitten aside. "Why are you talking like that?" she asked. "Why are your words so mumbled?"

The Wizard opened his mouth and pointed at it.

Thud's jaw dropped. "You don't have any teeth!" she realised.

The Wizard pointed at Bard. The rooster covered his toothy beak.

Blunder pointed at the toothy rooster. "You stole the old man's teeth?!" he cried. "That is **SO EVIL!**"

"He stole from me first!" Bard said. He aimed a wing just over the Wizard's shoulder. "See? That's my **Golden Harp** floating in the air!"

Blunder leveled his sword at the Wizard. "Then clearly you are the Evil one!" he cried.

The Wizard shrugged. "He tuhnt people into theep!"

Bard helpfully translated for Thud and Blunder. "He said that he's guilty!" the rooster crowed. "You should beat him up right now."

Blunder raised his sword. "For justice!" he cried as he prepared to charge.

Thud grabbed him by the collar. "Hold your horses," she said. "I don't think that's what the Wizard said at all."

Bard locked his beady eyes onto Blunder's and pointed a wing at Thud. "Don't listen to her!" Bard said. "The Evil Wizard has clearly cast an Evil Spell on her! She can't be trusted!"

Blunder narrowed his eyes at his friend. "Thud . . . are you evil?"

Thud sighed. "No," she said.

Bard slyly slipped his wing around Blunder's shoulders. "But how can we trust her?" he cooed into his ear. "If she has been brainwashed, then she wouldn't know it!"

Blunder blinked at Bard. He blinked at Thud. "Um," he said.

Thud clenched her jaw. "Who's the one yelling and screaming like an Evil person, Blunder?" she said, gritting her teeth.

Blunder looked at Bard. "You are kind of scream-y," he said.

Bard waved his wing dismissively. "Don't let her calm, logical answers fool you! She –"

The Evil Wizard grabbed Bard by his chicken legs. He flipped him upside-down and held him dangling in the air.

With his free hand, the Evil Wizard grabbed Bard's teeth – and yanked them from his mouth.

Blunder's eyes went wide with terror. "You tore out his teeth?!" he cried. "That is **SO EVIL!**"

The Wizard shoved the teeth into his own mouth. "Much better," he said.

Blunder's eyes went even wider with even more terror.

"What kind of Evil person wears someone else's teeth?!" he cried.

"They're my false teeth," the Wizard said. He smiled, showing the rows of pearly whites. "See?"

Blunder's eyes were no longer wide. "Oh," he said. "I knew that."

CHAPTER 4

POULTRUS REVERSUS

The Wizard released Bard. The rooster spun in the air and landed on his feet. He raised a clenched wing in anger at the Wizard.

"This is all your fault!" Bard said. "You turned me into a rooster!"

The Wizard bent over and shook his fist at the rooster. "You took my teeth!" he said.

"Because you stole my **Golden Harp!**" Bard said.

"You kept misspelling with it!" the Wizard said.

"Because you stepped on it and broke it!" Bard said.

"You left it laying around!" the Wizard said.

Bard and the Wizard were nose-to-nose and growling, which was kind of weird because of the big size difference.

Thud pushed them apart. "Enough!" she cried. The two of them stared at Thud. "It sounds to me like you're both a little Evil," Thud said, crossing her arms. "Right, Blunder?"

Blunder didn't respond. Thud glanced over her shoulder. The heroic warrior was giggling and playing with the Evil Monsters.

"Good kitties," Blunder purred.

"BLUNDER!" Thud growled.

Blunder leapt to his feet and surveyed the scene. "The Evil Wizard's defences are down!" he cried. He lifted his sword and charged at the Wizard!

Thud held out one arm. **PLOK!** Blunder's forehead smacked into her palm, stopping him in his tracks.

Thud glowered at Bard and the Wizard. "If you two don't settle this argument," she said, "then I'll let *him* settle it!"

The Wizard and Bard eyed Blunder nervously. They glanced at each other. Both of them frowned.

The Wizard fidgeted with his beard. "I guess I'm sorry for turning you into a rooster," he said to Bard.

Bard crossed his wings. "And?" he asked.

The Wizard glared down at him. "And for stepping on your harp," he said.

Bard uncrossed his wings. "I'm sorry, too," he said. "It's my fault those villagers got turned into sheep."

The Wizard added, "But the singing cows and flying pigs were my fault."

Bard hung his head. "No, that was my fault, too," he said. "I stole your teeth, remember? You wouldn't have misspelled otherwise."

The Wizard smiled. "But you wouldn't have misspelled if I hadn't broken your harp," he said.

Bard grinned. "Then I guess we're both a little Evil," he said.

The Wizard nodded excitedly. "Yeah!" he said. He rubbed his chin. "Just a little."

The Not-so-Evil Wizard held out his hand. "Truce?" he asked.

Bard held out a wing. "Truce," he said. They shook on it.

"Good work, you two!" Thud said. She let go of Blunder's head. He crashed to the floor with a **THUD!**

"What gives, Thud?" Blunder said, rubbing his noggin.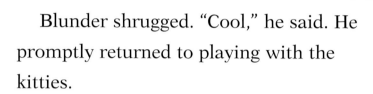

Thud helped her friend back to his feet. "I'll fill you in later," she said.

Blunder shrugged. "Cool," he said. He promptly returned to playing with the kitties.

Bard poked the Wizard with a wing. "Should we fix our misspellings now?"

"We'd really appreciate it," Thud said.

The Wizard nodded. "I'll go first," he said. He closed his eyes, waved his fingers in Bard's general direction, and chanted, **"Poultrus Reversus!"**

POOF! A puff of smoke surrounded Bard. A moment later, the smoke disappeared to reveal a boy.

Then the Wizard reached into the air, grabbed the Golden Harp, and handed it to Bard.

The boy's smile grew wider as he examined the musical instrument. "It's fixed!" he said.

The Wizard nodded. "I was going to apologise. And give it back," he said. "You know . . . before you stole my false teeth."

Bard frowned. "I'm sorry for taking your teeth . . . Dad."

They hugged. Thud made a funny face. "Wait a second," she said. "You're his father?!"

The Wizard nodded. "Didn't Bard tell you?" he said.

Thud glared at Bard. The rooster-turned-boy looked in the other direction and whistled innocently.

Thud cradled her face in her palm and shook her head. "You guys are so weird," she mumbled.

Then she looked up at them and said, "Now one of you needs to turn Village Town back to normal. Even though the pigs enjoy flying and the cows like singing, the villagers are surely tired of being sheep."

Bard and the Wizard met eyes. "Together?" the Wizard asked his son.

Bard nodded. "Together."

The Wizard held his hands in the air and wiggled his fingers. **"Sheepus Reversus!"** he chanted.

Bard strummed his Golden Harp. **"Guernsey Returnsey!"** he sang.

Bard and the Wizard leaned close. As one, they said, **"Oinkers Yoinkers!"**

Not too far away, in Village Town, the villagers were quite happy to be back to normal. The pigs and cows, however, were terribly sad.

"Everything back to normal?" Thud asked. The two magical friends nodded.

Blunder smiled. "Nice work, Thud," he said. "Can we go slay some monsters now?"

Thud grinned. "Is the sky blue?" she asked.

Blunder thought for a moment. "Yes!" he eventually said.

"HE-HE-HE!" Thud giggled.

The Wizard smiled a toothy smile. "Hey, Thud and Blunder . . . can we come with you?"

Bard gripped his harp. "Oh, please! Can we?" he begged. "We love adventure! And we can cast really cool spells!"

Thud rubbed her chin. "On one condition. You both must promise to stop being Evil," she said. "Not even a little bit Evil."

The Wizard and Bard nodded excitedly. "We promise!" they said together.

Thud and Blunder held their weapons above their heads.

"To victory!" Blunder cried.

"And battle!" Thud added.

Blunder sighed. "I got it backward again, didn't I?" he asked.

Thud punched him in the shoulder. "Sounded pretty good to me," she said.

Wizard stretched his fingers. "Ready, my son?"

"Let's cock-a-doodle do it!" Bard cried.

Talk About the Tale!

1. What things does Bard do throughout the book that show he may not be whom he says he is?

2. What do you think the Magical Transportation Device would be called in our world?

3. How did Bard and the Evil Wizard settle their argument?

Write About the Adventure!

1. Do you think it was okay for Bard to steal the Evil Wizard's teeth just because he'd stolen Bard's Golden Harp? Why or why not?

2. Thud is more cautious than Blunder, who often acts without thinking first. Who are you more like and why?

3. What or who do you think the Wildest Turkey turned back into after the spell was reversed?

GLOSSARY

adventurer   anyone who looks for adventure and danger and Evil, with a capital *E*

bitter   to be angry and hurt, especially at an evil wizard after he turned you into a barnyard animal

crater   a large hole in the ground; run if it was made by a monster with a spiked club!

eerie   strange and frightening, like an evil wizard

fidget   to make small, quick, nervous movements

intruder   a person who enters a place where he or she is unwanted, like sneaking into an evil wizard's tower without an invite

justice   punishment for doing something wrong, like poking someone with a pointy sword

portal   an entrance or opening

prompt   immediate, without delay, like right NOW!

smite   to strike someone, possibly with a sword, hammer or some sort of spiked weapon

truce   an agreement to stop fighting; truces are best made when you are out of breath or hungry for a snack

ABOUT THE CREATORS

ABOUT the AUTHOR

Author Sean Tulien works as a book editor in Seattle, Washington. In his free time, Sean likes to read, eat sushi, exercise outdoors, listen to loud music, play with his quirky bunny, Habibi, and his curious hamster, Buddy, and spend time with his brilliant wife, Nicolle. When he's not doing all that stuff, Sean loves to write books like this one.

ABOUT the ILLUSTRATOR

 Illustrator Pol Cunyat was born in 1979 in Sant Celoni, a small village near Barcelona, Spain. As a child, Pol always dreamed of being an illustrator. So he went to study illustration in Escola De Còmic Joso de Barcelona and Escola D'Art, Serra i Abella de L'Hospitalet. Now, Pol makes a living doing illustration work for various publishers and studios. Pol's dream has come true, but he will never stop dreaming.